The Amazing Hidden Talents of Anibabs...

BUBBLES

For my dad who was the most amazing storyteller.
He filled my head with awe and wonder,
making everything that seemed impossible, possible.

For more information contact reading@anibabs.com
ISBN: 9798561486050

What amazing things have you done today?

Inside of me
And inside of you,
There is something amazing
That we can do.

You might not know it,
Your body hasn't shown it,
But there is something amazing
We all can do.

Anibabs, the girl who
Lives next door,
Didn't have a clue
Until she turned four.

That's when it started,
It wasn't any trouble,
She just discovered,
That she could...

BLOW BUBBLES!

Now I don't mean the normal ones
You blow from a wand,
Or the ones from your mouth
That you roll with your tongue,
It's a very rare talent,
Don't you fear,

For Anibabs could blow
Bubbles from her...

Big ones, small ones,
Ones with holes in the middle,
Out they popped
In a peculiar muddle!
Long ones, short ones,
Teeny ones galore,
Popping from her ears,
More, more and more!

Bubbles of all colours,
Pink, yellow, blue,
Bubbles of all shapes
Can you believe it?

It's true!

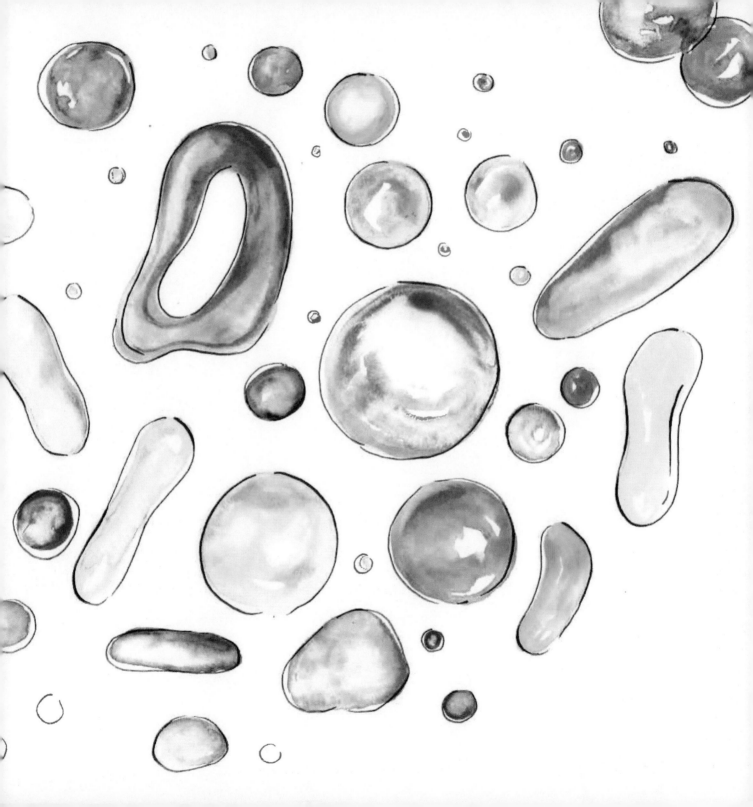

Squares and circles,
Diamonds and cubes,
Ovals and triangles
And cylinder tubes,

Twirling and whirling
And dancing in the light,
Anibabs' bubbles
Popped throughout the night!

What a vision! What a sight!
Anibabs are you alright?
For just then as she reached,
Down to her toes,

More bubbles began to pop,
But this time from her...

Nose!

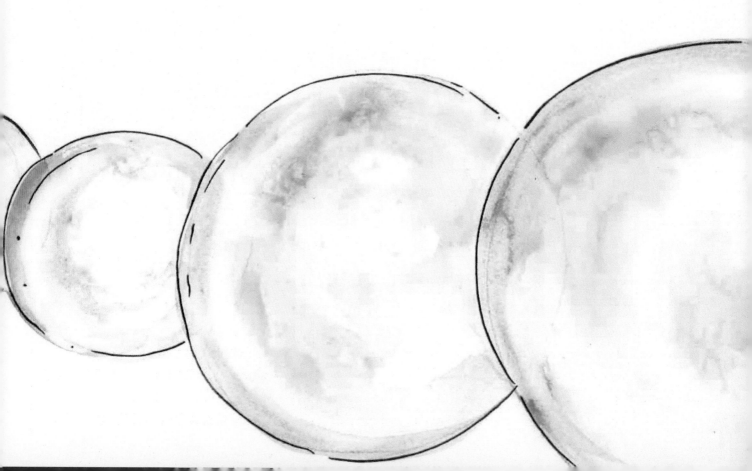

Out burst bubbles,
Of different kinds of fruit,
Bananas, apples,
A melon or two.

Strawberries, kiwi,
A big bunch of grapes,
They looked so delicious
I tried to catch them on a plate!

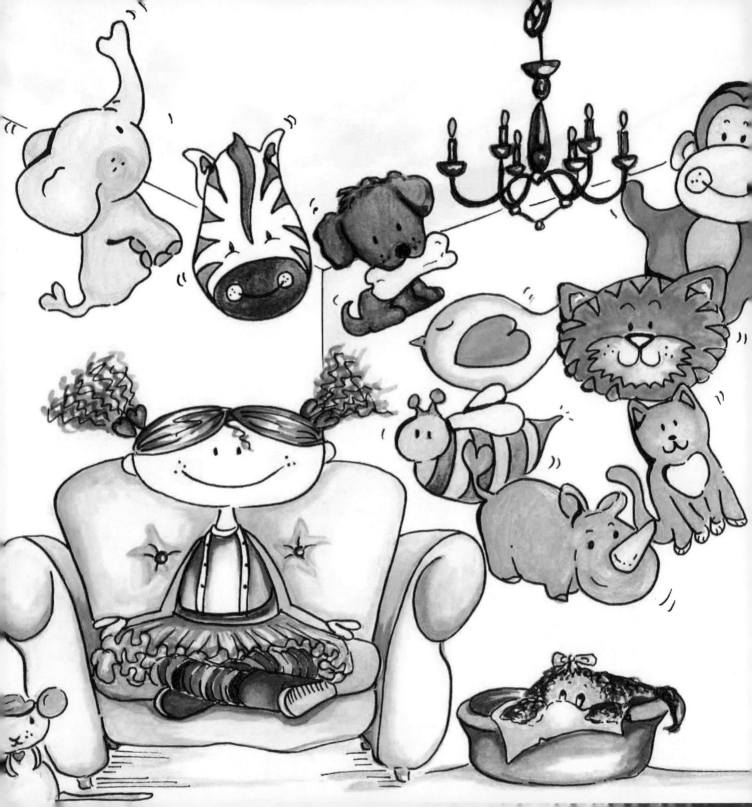

Next came the animals,
A dog and a cat,
I think I even saw a mouse,
Wearing a hat!

A tiger, an elephant,
A zebra and a bee,
A bird and a rhino,
Wow,
A cheeky monkey!

Amazing, amazing,
Anibabs you are,
Then right before
My very eyes
She blew out
Shooting stars!

With her eyes shut tight
And not making any sound,
Out shot more bubbles
Flying high above the ground.

Car bubbles,
Bike bubbles,
A bubble of a
train,
It sped so fast
out of her nose
Being chased by
a plane!

It truly is amazing,
The talent of this girl,
A talent she never knew
she had,
You could give it a whirl!

There really is not much,
More that I can say,
Until early this morning
As she went on her way,

Anibabs had a rumbling,
Deep in her tum,
And oh wow more bubbles,
Popped out of her...

Bum!

So always remember that...

Inside of me,
And inside of you,
There is something amazing
We all can do!

Can you...

Pull a funny face?   Hop?   Write a number?

Be kind?   Touch your toes?   Sing?

You are amazing!

A note from the author...

Hi there! I hope you enjoyed sharing this book with a little one!
Reading can really help to open up the imagination of our children and
should always be a happy experience.

As well as being fun, the story covers many
opportunities to learn, or reinforce, the names of
shapes, colours, animals, fruits and vehicles
with lots of rhyming words to find.

Anibabs has unique talents, we are all
different and we all face our own
challenges.
The story can lead to a celebration
of the amazing things our children
can achieve, whether it be putting
on their shoes, or learning a
new number; it is a chance to
set new, amazing goals and
encourage them in every little
step they take.

If you enjoyed 'Bubbles' then look
out for two more amazing titles in
The Amazing Hidden Talents of Anibabs
series, and check out her website
for lots of free activities and
fun stuff to do!

www.anibabs.com
reading@anibabs.com
If you could leave a positive
review on Amazon then that
would be an Amazing thing to do!

Printed in Great Britain
by Amazon

82840408R00020